SOUTH WEST TALES

Edited By Sarah Washer

First published in Great Britain in 2018 by:

 Young**Writers**

Young Writers
Remus House
Coltsfoot Drive
Peterborough
PE2 9BF
Telephone: 01733 890066
Website: www.youngwriters.co.uk

FOREWORD

Young Writers was created in 1991 with the express purpose of promoting and encouraging creative writing. Each competition we create is tailored to the relevant age group, hopefully giving each pupil the inspiration and incentive to create their own piece of work, whether it's a poem or a short story. We truly believe that seeing their work in print gives pupils a sense of achievement and pride in their work and themselves.

For Stranger Sagas, we challenged secondary school pupils to write a mini saga – a story in just 100 words. They were given the choice of eight story starters to give their imaginations a kick start:

- At birth everyone's tattooed with their date of death. Mine's dated yesterday...
- The last thing I remember is...
- I unravel the family portrait; if these are my parents, who's that downstairs...?
- I need to tell someone the truth before it's too late...
- The sun was blazing; I took out the map, I must be close...
- There was a noise coming from the basement...
- We watched from the space station as Earth exploded...
- I got off the plane, the terminal was empty...

They could use any one of these to begin their story, or alternatively they could choose to go it alone and create that all important first line themselves. With bizarre beginnings, mysterious middles and enigmatic endings, the resulting tales in this collection cover a range of genres and showcase the talent of the next generation. From fun to frightening to the weird and wonderful, these mini sagas are sure to keep you entertained and take you to strange new worlds.

CONTENTS

Chloe Jessica Harris (12)	68
Reece Pierce (14)	69
Abbie Faulkner (13)	70
Emma Brown (12)	71
Owen Forster (12)	72
Rosie Thistlewood (12)	73
Izzy Reece (14)	74
Kaitlyn McFarlane (12)	75
Tia Kirwin (13)	76
Emily Barrow (13)	77
Nicole Knight (14)	78
Jared Lancaster (14)	79
Samuel Joseph Huckle (13)	80
Pavel Sorocean (11)	81
Eden Boorman (14)	82
Lili Boon (12)	83
Lewis Giles (13)	84
Lotti Heathcote (12)	85
Rosie Egerton (11)	86
Darcy Philip McBride (12)	87
Rhys Hall (13)	88
Samuel Evans-Murray (14)	89
Ashleigh Jennings (12)	90
Dylan James Gould (14)	91
Caitlin Chessell (12)	92
Bradley Morris (13)	93
Lily Copeland (12)	94
Velimira Radoeva Ekova (12)	95
Erin Leah Longford (13)	96
Oliver Taylor (14)	97
Josh Fifield (12)	98
Tom Edgecombe (13)	99
Oliver Thomas Baugh (11)	100
Cerys Dickinson (13)	101
Maddy McPhee (12)	102
Bethany Marie McPhee (14)	103
Patrick Middle (12)	104
Jude Van Manton (13)	105
Jack Goring (12)	106
Callum Edisbury-Bell (14)	107
Toby Ambridge (13)	108
Benjamin Van Der Helstraete (11)	109

Tilly May Butler (13)	110
Esme Sheath (13)	111
Freddie Cox (12)	112
Anya Wright (13)	113
Kade Woodford (12)	114
James Thompson (12)	115
Luke Felstead (14)	116
Liam Parkman (14)	117
James Boxx (12)	118
Lucie Hayden (13)	119
Steve Edgcombe (11)	120
Joshua Wilson (12)	121
Finn Mahoney (12)	122
Rose Robinson (12)	123
Jacob Kennesion (12)	124
Isobel Irene Cole (13)	125
Molly Carter (13)	126
Nakita Eleanor Munn (13)	127
Rylan Agius Schembri (13)	128
Mia Topping (12)	129
Megon Blow (12)	130
Kira Plant (13)	131

King Edward VI Community College, Totnes

Bea Jane (12)	132
Freya Kissane Dilloway Cashman (12)	133
Emma Tibbetts (12)	134
Ella Wyett (13)	135

St Wilfrid's School, Exeter

Alden Landis Tabor (11)	136
David Antwi (12)	137
George Nicholas Sparey (12)	138
Tim Allison (14)	139
Olivia Richardson (11)	140
Christian Tigwell (12)	141

The John Of Gaunt School, Trowbridge

THE MINI SAGAS

Mouth Sealed With Secrets

I need to tell someone... Jacob is the killer. Can I keep this secret any longer? He killed my sister? She was all I had left. I'll tell Jessica...

Two days later... "How could you keep this from us?" hospital manager, Jean, exclaimed.

But Jacob was my friend. I didn't want to stitch him up. "I'm sorry," I replied bitterly.

"If you can't keep a secret to yourself don't expect others to!" Jean complained.

I sat there in silence. Silence. I felt hated... I can't trust Jessica any more but I'm just as guilty. Just as thoughtless as Jacob...

Jessie Griffin (12)

Buckler's Mead Academy, Yeovil

Separation

My little brother screaming in pain and faint outlines of men. It's not clear enough yet. It's just a blur. This looks like District Four, that's impossible, I live in Seven. Or lived! The Death Star must have come. But why me?

"There's someone over here," shouted a man with a deep voice. The man came into sight with a bat.

"Excuse me, is there anyone else here?" I murmured.

He lifted the bat and swung it at my head. "That will hurt in the morning," he whispered.

Then I saw my brother screaming in pain again. Separation and isolation...

Larna Simpson (12)
Buckler's Mead Academy, Yeovil

The Midnight Disaster

"Dad, what are you doing?" asked Martha.

"Oh nothing, I'm just going through all of the family photos. Care to join me?" David, Martha's dad, had always been a bit strange. Whenever Martha walked past, she would always get a sly look from him.

"Umm... yeah sure," said Martha. She walked into the attic. Her dad left the room and went downstairs. The time was 11.59. Martha found a picture that was covered in dust. She paused. She unravelled the family portrait... "If these are my parents, then who is that downstairs?"

Grace Whatmore (12)
Buckler's Mead Academy, Yeovil

The Mystery

So carefully and cautiously I walk down the creaky, wooden stairs. I hear very faint whispering. There are two people dressed in black. I couldn't quite get a clear insight on the two suspects. However I creep a bit closer so I can peer my head around the door... They've gone! They've vanished like the speed of lightning. I carefully and anxiously walk slowly into the kitchen to find a frightening note. 'Be aware of the ghost frighteners'. I jumped out of my skin. I was totally freaked out. I couldn't believe my eyes. Is this the end?

Harry Richard Wiles (11)
Buckler's Mead Academy, Yeovil

Hello, Listen To This

"I was walking to the shop through the forest trail. I was getting some shopping, after that is a blur..." the man said. "How did I get here?"

"Five long days ago, four coma patients vanished like that. One male, two women and one child. They were all admitted to us at the same time. One man claimed to have been walking to the shop. The coma patient's walking, alive and well."

He turned the TV off. "What do you think happened?"

"I will just say, no one is safe from you, me or all of them."

Miles Lewin (13)
Buckler's Mead Academy, Yeovil

Who Is That?

As usual I was sitting in my favourite game, Bubble Shooter. Suddenly someone called my name to come downstairs but it wasn't my parents (they were out). So I hid under my bed so I couldn't be seen.

There it was, that creepy, ghostly voice was calling me. It was saying, "Sophie I've got something for you."

I rushed downstairs and went into the kitchen and there it was, a person with her back to me. The door slammed open and I said, "If they're my parents, then who's that in the kitchen?"...

Marissa Buckle (12)
Buckler's Mead Academy, Yeovil

The House In The Alleyway

So my friends dared me to enter this building which no one ever comes out from when they enter. They never thought it was true! I entered a little alleyway and it was as spooky as a Halloween nght. I turned my head and it was there. There was a sign saying: *Danger but enter if you dare.* I climbed over the fence and entered the house.

On the news: "We have now heard from the boy's friends that he entered the strange building alone and nobody ever comes out from this horrible building hidden behind the trees..."

Keisha James (13)
Buckler's Mead Academy, Yeovil

Secrets!

I had a secret. Now this secret killed people. My whole life was based on a secret that I held closest to my heart. School was terrible, everybody walking around like they had murdered someone. Well many people wouldn't believe this but I have, and I regret pushing Nancy off that cliff. I hadn't told anybody but I felt like people knew. I was left out nobody liked me; exiled from society but nobody else knew somebody helped me do it. He was popular and the maker of my unpopularity. I hate him but now somebody must know the truth.

Elizabeth Faulkner (12)
Buckler's Mead Academy, Yeovil

I Need To Tell The Truth

Bang! What was that...? Do I get out and look or do I stay here? *Bang!* There it was again. It was me, I got shot in the leg... Who would shoot me? Then I saw it. A person in a black coat, a tall white man. I needed to tell someone the truth before it was too late... It's about the gunner. I tried to stem the bleeding, I called for help but no answer. *Smash!* The glass window shattered. People were screaming for help. I needed to tell the truth. I could hear people running, shouting, "Get down!"

Elena Kirkpatrick (14)
Buckler's Mead Academy, Yeovil

The Morning Confusion

I woke up and as usual, my dad was downstairs having breakfast, in the basement. He was making a very strange noise whilst having breakfast. I wasn't ready for breakfast, so I decided to clean my room. As I was going through all my photos I came across a picture of my dad... It was slightly suspicious. So I went downstairs to the basement and showed my dad... "Dad!" There was no sign of dad. So I got to the top of the stairs and suddenly I had a thought, *if that's my dad, then who's that downstairs?*

Holly Richards (12)
Buckler's Mead Academy, Yeovil

Little Red Riding Hood

One day, Little Red Riding Hood was walking through the woods to go and see her grandmother. She had picked some bluebells and daisies for her. As she walked through the door to her grandmother's house, all was fine until she handed the old lady her flowers, then her body started shaking. Suddenly, she ran to the bathroom. Within a flash she had turned into a wolf. At that moment she remembered, when she was little the girl was cursed. When she grew up to be a woman she would turn into a wolf. She needed to tell someone...

Charlotte Bant (11)
Buckler's Mead Academy, Yeovil

The Meteor

We watched from the space station as Earth exploded. We'd been watching it for years, twenty years to be exact. At first we'd thought it would avoid Earth but then, about five years in, it changed course and headed straight for it. All the world leaders were assembled to decide what to do. It was half the size of the world. There was nothing we could do to save it, so it was decided we were going to build rockets that would go into space and build a space station with everything we would need to survive the meteor!

Tyler Stevenson (13)
Buckler's Mead Academy, Yeovil

Forgotten Past

I have to keep the truth. The truth that scares me when I'm awake. Nobody knows about it apart from me. I can't believe that I made myself a liar. I took away important information that everybody needs to know. Every day I keep thinking and it makes my heart beat faster than usual. Many questions around my head that I want to forget. I am desperate to get out of this life that made me different from everyone around. The last thing I can remember is, I need to change my life and just keep the horrible truth behind.

Deane Alvarez (13)
Buckler's Mead Academy, Yeovil

The Last Word Heard Was...

Hello! I turned round and there was a person speaking but I could not hear a word they were saying. I was all alone in the dark listening to music. I'd taken out one of my earplugs but couldn't hear a word they were saying. She was wearing an elf outfit. She had all the features of a real elf. Her teeth were as pointy as shark teeth! The colour of her eyes was like strawberries. Slowly the elves started to walk closer to me. From their necks up, everything was moving! She quickly hugged me, squeezing me tight...

Millie Nicole Tucker (11)
Buckler's Mead Academy, Yeovil

Fear

When I woke up there was an eerie feeling in my bones. A few hours later I went to my usual social spot; the edge of the dark forest. There I met up with my gorgeous boyfriend, Noah, and we made a blazing bonfire. Suddenly, I heard snaps from branches coming from the forest. Both Noah and I investigated but the only trace was a golden locket with 'fear' engraved into it. *Bang!* A gunshot flew up into the cloudy sky. I sprinted deeper into the trees and let the darkness penetrate everything. I was alone.

Florence Bower (12)
Buckler's Mead Academy, Yeovil

The Girl In The Basement

There was nothing I could do but freeze; hoping it was just my imagination. My parents were out so I knew it wasn't them. I was in the bathroom getting out of the shower; it sounded like it was coming from the basement. I wanted to get Dad's ladder but if he found out he would go... *Boom!* I heard it again and I stopped thinking about that and got it. Slowly I opened the lock and looked down. Standing there was a girl giving me a sinister look. I could see the end. She smiled then ran towards me...

Jamie Bisset (12)
Buckler's Mead Academy, Yeovil

Death Comes

All I remembered was dying; cheery I know. Friday 13th. Typical. It had to be me. Cursed forever. I died yesterday. I woke up and thought, *I'm still dead aren't I?* It was not supposed to be like this. He didn't tell me! Never mind, I suppose I'd better get used to it. I would never forget what happened. I reached out. I took it. Biggest regret of my life. I put it in my mouth. I felt the crunch as the pill broke into pieces. I felt dizzy. I fainted. I never woke up again. Take my advice!

Kiera Evans (12)

Buckler's Mead Academy, Yeovil

Cult Of Santas

I knew the aliens were coming. They might already be here. They may have always been here. Nobody would ever believe me, but I knew, I knew the aliens were always here. As every famous person in history, collecting data. They always seemed to be close with a person of the same traits to others of the same. I was every one of them. Being reincarnated over and over again. I came to the broken house where I knew the aliens were. Where I expected to see five aliens, I found five Santas. A cult, as such, of Santas...

George Bennett (13)
Buckler's Mead Academy, Yeovil

The Basement

There was a tapping sound, slow and then fast. Fear crept inside of me, myths of the village playing around in my head. Were they true? A low musty voice called my name. Nobody knew me around here. I heard the familiar creak of the door. Then footsteps came to me. I ran towards it screaming, crying. A pain shot in my forehead. I fell. I died. Sweat dripped down me. I was revived. I was alive. I was told I tripped but I didn't. There was something black with red eyes on the basement stairs; nothing added up.

Caitlyn Richards (12)
Buckler's Mead Academy, Yeovil

The Death Date

At birth everyone is tattooed with their death date. Mine was yesterday. How is this possible? It was clear on my wrist, January 1st 1926. I looked away then looked again... Same date. Suddenly my mum walked in with tears streaming down her face. "Mum, what's wrong?" I whispered.

My mum ignored me and walked over to the window.

"Mum," I called again. I slowly got up to comfort her and reached out my arms to hug her but she didn't react. It was like I was not even there...

Maizie Bond (12)
Buckler's Mead Academy, Yeovil

The Last Thing I Remember Is...

... the screaming of my parents as I fell to the ground! It was 12 o'clock and Christmas night. Everywhere was dark but I could hear noises coming from downstairs. I had never believed in Santa before so it had to be something else. Slowly I tiptoed down the stairs and peered through the glass in the door and, to my disbelief, there was a little man in a red and white suit. He turned round and stared. It wasn't Santa! I didn't know what it was but I looked in its eyes and dropped to the floor...

Charlotte Harmer (12)
Buckler's Mead Academy, Yeovil

The Death In The Basement

There was a noise coming from the basement. I opened the door slowly. I walked down step by step ever so slowly. There was a rumble of wood at the bottom of the stairs. I heard a scream. I wandered the endless maze of lost and forgotten junk. There was a rope and chair. I heard a snap. I heard a voice: "I'm here." There was a dress. I heard footsteps all around me. The walking turned into running. There was a shadow looming and there was a noise coming from the basement. I opened the door...

Jonathan Lock (13)
Buckler's Mead Academy, Yeovil

Mystery Death Date

It must be wrong. What if it isn't? I don't want my life to end. I'm only young. I can feel my neck hairs stand. *Am I the first person to live past their expected death date? Am I going to die today or going to survive? Is this all fake and you die whenever your body wants to?* All these thoughts rushed through my head and made me feel more scared. I never knew why we had a tattoo of our death date. "I need to find out why I'm still alive," I whisper. "But how?"

Livvy Orchard (12)
Buckler's Mead Academy, Yeovil

The Fence Goes On Forever And Ever

It's pitch-black. "Hey Fred, get over here, try and climb over the fence so that you can unlock the door!"
"Okay, I'm over. I will open the gate."
We went into what we thought was an abandoned runway, but as we walked on, we saw a hanger. I looked inside and there was a plane. We looked inside and we saw a dead body. We were horrified. I heard a noise. I looked at the back of the plane. I looked down every row and saw a man at the back. Then he started to run...

Eddie Wright (13)
Buckler's Mead Academy, Yeovil

Before It Is Too Late

I can't keep it a secret forever... I went to my class the next day, I was anxious but ready. My teacher knew I needed to speak. Time was escaping. The teacher got the class settled and then I said it. I never thought I would actually say it to everyone. It felt good but bad at the same time. I have... Suddenly, I couldn't speak and I started shaking. There was a confusion. Quickly I ran out of the class and down to the main hall. I couldn't. From that day on I was never seen again...

Daisy Passmore (12)
Buckler's Mead Academy, Yeovil

The Curse That Changed My Life

The last thing I remember is backing into a corner and crying. I then woke up in the hospital with half of my arm missing. My mum said that she found me dangling from the bannister. She thought I was playing around until she saw the blood and the curved tooth. I went cold at the words 'curved tooth' it reminded me of what I saw in the newspaper. I got attacked by a demi-gorgon. I was surprised I survived. Then it hit me, my dad wasn't here. Then my mum told me my father got cursed...

Rhia Bayley (13)
Buckler's Mead Academy, Yeovil

The Extinction Of Mystic Island

I finally climbed out of the fighter jet, the military base was empty, there was a sound like a girl crying and screaming. I turned my head the slightest inch and the smell was horrible like a rotten corpse. Before I could find what the smell was, I got tackled to the ground and felt a huge chunk of skin being torn out of my leg. I screamed in agony. I managed to grab my gun from my pocket and before I knew it I had blood all over me. I looked into the distance and there was something there...

Jamie Lucas (13)
Buckler's Mead Academy, Yeovil

The Two Men

Being on the train on the way to France, I slowly open my eyes and look around. White walls surround me. I try to lift my arms but I can't. I look down and see a brown belt over them. Suddenly I hear a loud, annoying beep and see two men with a wheelchair. It screeches along the tiled floor, giving me a painful headache. As quick as a flash one of the men stab something into my arm.
I wake up, I have been tied down onto the wheelchair.
"Where am I?" I ask.
They laugh.

Nadia Gorczyca (13)
Buckler's Mead Academy, Yeovil

Adam's Mystery

There was a noise coming from the basement. Adam glared in fear as noises sounded from below. In distress Adam panicked. He went to get an axe from the shed. He came in the kitchen, the table was gone, the chairs were gone. Adam peered down into the basement. The door was open. Shivers ran down his spine. He tiptoed down the stairs of the frightening basement and noises could be heard! As darkness could be seen, the door creaked and Adam was petrified. The door slammed shut. It was a trap...

Josh Dey (11)
Buckler's Mead Academy, Yeovil

Mystery World

I saw a field and at the other end was the hotel I was staying at. Perhaps a shortcut? But no! I took one gentle step into the field and I was transported into another dimension. There were dragons and dinosaurs. I could see where I had to get out, but it would take days. A dragon walked over to me and started rubbing at my leg. That's when I knew what to do. It took me days to train him to fly with me but it finally worked. But the question is: Should I leave or should I stay?

Charlie Guppy (13)
Buckler's Mead Academy, Yeovil

Knocked-Over Chairs

The last thing I recall doing was hanging around, literally. Chairs knocked over, losing grip of reality, loved ones and myself. Voices were echoing, mind fading with the world around me descending. The black void surrounded, voices soon turning into cries for help and the atmosphere turning dead. Silence felt like it was crawling as the darkness took over the mental mind. Grasping for air, my body went as pale as snow and with the last breath, my mind went empty...

Billy-Joe Gumbleton (12)
Buckler's Mead Academy, Yeovil

The Noisy Basement

There was a noise coming from the basement and as I heard the noise I ran down to the basement as I thought my dad was back but he wasn't. "I don't know where the noise is coming from," I said to myself. As I turned around I saw a white sheet floating. I was petrified so I grabbed the sheet off the person and... *bang!*
It was just my dad trying to scare me. He was home and I was happy to see him because he'd been to war to fight.

Maisie Stafford (12)
Buckler's Mead Academy, Yeovil

The Shadow Man

I was thinking about that all night until someone turned up at my door. He had a black suit on with a black top hat and also he had a sharp knife in his hand. I panicked and jumped out the window that was wide open. Sprinting for my life, as I looked behind me I could see the man coming. He looked like he could run forever. Suddenly the path came to an end. It was a dead end. This was the end. This was it. He was getting closer and closer and closer...

Sam Bland (11)
Buckler's Mead Academy, Yeovil

Intruder

I slowly moved downstairs, I heard whispering from somewhere. I walked down the stairs but whenever I moved down a stair a loud creaking noise appeared from the stairs. When I finally got down all the stairs, a noise made me peep round the corner and I saw a mysterious man and then *poof!* he was gone. I slowly explored all the rooms and behind every corner then when I was at the end of the hallway I turned around and he was there...

Levi Boulton (11)
Buckler's Mead Academy, Yeovil

The Lucky Ones

I had somehow escaped the claws of death. I felt so lucky but I knew it wouldn't be long before they realised their mistake. I had to leave, but there was a force inside me that was saying I had to save my friends. I ran with my chains straining me down. As I reached the holding cell, I scaled the wall and I reached my friend who was more like family. That was three years ago, we were the lucky ones. Well, something like that at least.

Ethan Smalley (12)
Buckler's Mead Academy, Yeovil

Toxic Water

I wandered into the darkness of the airport. All of the shops were empty. My mind kept focusing on this growling sound which was very faint. No electric was on, I had no idea where I was or what time it was. I found a bloody sickle. The lights in the card shop turned on and my heart threw up at the top of my neck. The growling became more obnoxious and annoying. A horde of dead people lit up. Stack upon stack of bodies...

Lenny Mark Curwen (12)
Buckler's Mead Academy, Yeovil

Don't Look Away!

Looking out of my bedroom window from the corner of my eye I saw a man with a large bag on his head. As I looked in the dark for a second then back, he got closer, I tested him. I looked away and then back. He got closer, much closer. My heart started racing. I got out my phone and rang. I felt heavy breathing at the back of my neck. I turned around and he was standing there and he was just staring at me...

Brodie Ray Cox (12)
Buckler's Mead Academy, Yeovil

Blade

There was a noise coming from the basement... it sounded like an alien in distress. Blade went to the garage and grabbed a knife. He opened the door. It creaked with a chilling silence. The silence followed him. He crept down the stairs and to his surprise... There was a tall alien. It had dark grey skin. Blade went and stabbed him in the back. It then turned round...

Callum Rice (11)

Buckler's Mead Academy, Yeovil

Insanity Is Immortality

The lights are blinking, screeching. Thoughts scatter through my mind. Trepidation grasps me. Metal tendrils clasp my wrists. Why aren't I breathing? I remember his face. The crinkled, pallid complexion contrasting with his piercing eyes as if concentrated tenebrosity had been poured into them. His beam shrouds his visage with false emotions. I remember him telling me that the fingers of the tenebrous disease had grasped my mind; that I had tripped off the surface of reality. Then, where am I? Searing pain enveloped my forehead. My vision blurred. The lights flickered out of focus. Obscurity blanketed my mind...

Beth Cobden (14)
Cowes Enterprise College, Cowes

The Last Thing I Remember Was...

... gunfire. The floor swayed and swerved and spiralled from underneath my feet. So much that I had been unable to stand. I don't remember anything after that. Now, I'm trapped in a dark room with no light except a single flickering candle. The floor was cold, the room was silent and the smell was disgusting. Then a blinding light shone throughout the room as a tall, silver-haired woman entered. She stared at me, analysing my every feature. "You don't strike me as a professional criminal," she stated in a tedious voice.

"That's what makes me so good at it."

Grace Boulton (12)
Cowes Enterprise College, Cowes

Death Dates

Everyone has a day where they'll meet their demise. Having it tattooed on your wrist makes you paranoid. My death date was yesterday, 30th December except I'm still alive. Why? What have I done differently. Everyone I know died on their death dates. My mum died two weeks ago. I wasn't that upset it was expected. You could tell she was dying just by looking at her. However I still seemed healthy besides some abnormalities I'd begun to notice about myself. Some physical and some psychological; such as the ability to see the dead, and super intelligence which is odd...

Talitha Scofield (13)
Cowes Enterprise College, Cowes

Year 2091 - Rehelm Station. Abolishment Of Earth 8pm GMT

We watched from the space station as Earth exploded; the disease has been conquered. We were warned, but were ignorant of such things. If we'd listened then the world could have continued to thrive. However, it seemed from the minute Specimen C36 was aboard... the world was already destined for annihilation. Seventeen years earlier... I stepped down from the bridge onto the central lift of the Pandora, all the time I've invested will pay off. I finally found a specimen of life from its surface... I will go down in history as the one that saved humanity, fame and glory!

Harry Keith (13)
Cowes Enterprise College, Cowes

Untitled

There it is. A great tower of limestone, colossal even to the Sahara itself. My inheritance. My lab. Inside I find my worker drones buzzing around. They keep the place in order. They're not what I'm looking for though. Upstairs, my fabrication room waits for me, clean and polished hoping for a task. I give it a sword to duplicate and leave. It's not what I'm looking for. This however is. On the roof at the top, the mountain's summit the great platform stands, the shell. A hulking island-shaped, tortoise-legged robot. That's my home. My noble kingdom...

Nathaniel Jones (13)
Cowes Enterprise College, Cowes

My Last Thought...

I unravel the family portrait; if these are my parents, who's downstairs? The clock struck midnight, almost making me jumped out of my skin. Various questions dashed around my head. Who was that downstairs? Is he dangerous? My heart beat faster, like it was going to bust out of my chest. I suddenly heard a noise, a creak. I then heard loud, echoing footsteps. Somebody or something was walking up the stairs. My breathing got heavier, making me feel light-headed. Then the door started opening and the last thought that went through my head was, *I'm trapped.*

Illeana Taylor-Burns (13)

Cowes Enterprise College, Cowes

Lockdown

The window blew open. The lockdown alarm continued and echoed throughout the school. We turned the lights off, put the blinds down, all huddling against the wall. A bang came from the corridors. We all did the drills. We joked about them but this time it was real. We heard boots coming along the corridor. Someone was coming closer and closer. He came, he walked past our door. He was holding something in his hand. He walked on but then he turned and faced the door, then a loud bang...

"No more today class. We'll read some more tomorrow. Dismissed!"

Daisy Coward (12)
Cowes Enterprise College, Cowes

The Serum

My colourful clothes gave away my obvious location. I leaned over the pebbled hill to uncover their secret. Chickens, pigs, even wolves were being injected with the dino DNA serum, which people thought did not exist anymore. I now realised that my mouth couldn't keep shut. In an instant, the chicken grew wings, wings that could fly! It was at this moment where my body reacted.
"Do not move!" I heard a deep voice yell out as fear filled my stomach.
I needed to escape. The world suddenly felt distant as blood cascaded from my head. I was dead.

Luke Woolston (13)
Cowes Enterprise College, Cowes

Nature Took Over

I got off the plane, the terminal was empty. The desks were empty. However as I got outside New York was not. Plants entwined around the buildings looking as though they had revenge. I could see, in the distance, a rhino-looking creature glanced into the deserted cars that seemed to look like a trail of dead bodies. I heard no construction sounds or bustling people rushing to catch a bus. Only the sound of animals rustling through the leaves. I started to panic. Something had changed in New York. Something big. Almost anyone could have seen. Nature fought back...

Evelynn King (12)
Cowes Enterprise College, Cowes

The Crumbling Land

The beautiful, cold, crisp and sunny day suddenly turned gloomy. Clouds slowly started creeping along the blue sky like a cheetah creeping towards its prey. Everywhere I went it was silent, apart from the occasional screech from a crow in fear as the sky vanished behind the clouds. But that wasn't the end... The weather started to become extreme sounding like rocks smashing against each other. There was no sign of life left. The crow had fallen silent. The land once full of life and colours slowly collapsed and plunged into darkness. Was this to be the end?

Jason Cass (13)
Cowes Enterprise College, Cowes

Aftermath

The world has been a blur my entire life but now it's dead. It's all nothing; a ball of nothing. Why did this happen? Just why? My family dead, my friends dead, nearly everyone dead. The cities wrecked; the economy gone. The remaining population, 2,000! That may seem like a lot but compared to 8,000,000,000 it's really nothing and to make it even worse, over half of them work for William Blitz. He's the man behind this global catastrophe. He takes everything, forcing us to scavenge, live life on the edge and worst of all, it makes us give up...

Jackson Hill (12)
Cowes Enterprise College, Cowes

We Watched From The Space Station As Earth Exploded

It was only one week after the event that they found Earth. Yet it took mere hours for it to fall. How is it possible? Wasn't Earth supposed to be humanity's one safe haven? Our military capital? Yet only three hours after the gorgons found it our navy was in ruins. Billions dead all because I had failed. I was on the London space station with Engineer Adams when I ordered the stealth systems to go offline for three seconds to cool the engines down. Instantly thousands of ships appeared shooting and bombing the hell out of us. Humanity's doomed...

Kieren Hawkewell (14)
Cowes Enterprise College, Cowes

Why Am I Not Dead?

At birth everyone's tattooed with their date of death. Mine's dated yesterday. That thought has been going through my head for what seems like eternity. I was searching through the library trying to find anything that could help. Once again it went through my head. Mine was dated yesterday. After hours of searching. I found nothing. I knew there was one hope left though. Someone, something could help me. Desmond Tiny! He was only a myth but my only hope. To my luck the myth was true and I found him quickly. What I found was horrifying. I was dead.

Adam Burt (13)
Cowes Enterprise College, Cowes

Why Is Always Me?

At birth everyone's tattooed with their date of death. Mine's dated yesterday. When I was only a baby my mother took me to an all boys' orphanage for troubled minds and homes. Because there was no letter or trace of my mother's existence they had no idea what age I was and that's where I think they got my death day muddled up. Just imagine it's a day before you die and your life is in God's hands at the age of eighteen. Christians believe in love and kindness, but this religion believes in keeping the world pure by killing...

Anwen Pugh (12)
Cowes Enterprise College, Cowes

The Ravages

The last phone left was crackling in an abandoned alley. Nearly all electrical equipment had been destroyed. A pool of blood had formed inside a deserted house. A half-eaten rotting corpse was lying inside it. A dishevelled hand reached for the phone - instead of using it the creature ate it. A year ago the virus spread; everyone over the age of sixteen had been infected. First it ravaged their brain, then it poisoned their heart. Now they roam the streets, famished and mad. They are the The Ravages and they can only eat the survivors... which is you!

Oscar Russell (12)
Cowes Enterprise College, Cowes

The Babysitter

I never thought that I would witness something like this. A murder, in my own house. Becky was downstairs with her friends dragging the body. "Laila get the book!" she said with a glare.

"Yes." She walked to a massive box in the corner of the room.

One of the friends was lying against the corpse doing funny things. They were acting like nothing happened. I ran into my room and slammed the door but then I heard a thud. I quietly snuck out of my room. I looked downstairs, all of the friends were lying on the floor... dead!

Isabella Pearson (11)
Cowes Enterprise College, Cowes

After Death Date

I scanned the surrounding area for clues but nothing seemed to fit. My mind pleaded for answers, trying to prevent what was about to happen. I slowly clutched his throat with my abnormal, ghostly fingers. His breath was vastly limited within my grasp and eventually his eyes lowered. Suddenly, a warping circle of glowing energy surrounded me, almost consuming me whole. The skies brightened with golden rays and I was sucked away from my current whereabouts. I felt bad about killing him but I had no choice - I had to, or else I could never ever leave.

Sonny Adams (14)
Cowes Enterprise College, Cowes

Run!

At birth everyone's tattooed with their date of death. Mine's dated yesterday. Catching my breath, I stopped, realising? What was I doing? Was this a mistake? I couldn't stop much longer or it would catch me. My heart was racing, my lungs gasping for breath, but I couldn't stop now. Not when I had got so much on the line. I kept saying to myself, "You can do this. You can do this!" But deep down I knew the truth. I knew that what I was running from could never be beaten. This beast always wins. I'm running from Death!

Jessica Gilbert (13)
Cowes Enterprise College, Cowes

Spy Sister

... was like elephants stomping in rage. I went down the stairs. I slowly looked round the corner and... There was my older sister for some strange reason. She was wearing... No, it can't be. But it is! A spy suit. I snuck in. She looked behind her and there I was. She said, "What are you doing here?" I replied, "There's someone at the front door."
We looked round the corner and there was her enemy. We snuck out the back, went round the front and saw him put a massive bomb outside. It blew the whole house up.

Shannon Attfield (13)
Cowes Enterprise College, Cowes

The Creature

The last thing I remember is running! Where am I? I feel different, almost un-human, what happened to me? I start walking through the bright green leaves of the forest. My body is burning, something's happening inside me. I feel like I'm changing, evolving. I look at my hands, scales! Suddenly a loud shriek consumes my hearing. Without thinking my body starts running. I can't stop. There's a clearing in the distance, where two little creatures bound up to me and lie by my side. A raindrop drops on a leaf near me. I look like them!

Reuben Reeves (13)
Cowes Enterprise College, Cowes

Will I Die?

If I don't die soon I'll get killed by the tribe leader. Leah was scared. She thought she'd be fine if she ran, if not she would die. She said to herself, "I'll run during the night and leave a note for my younger sister." That night, she wrote the letter and left. Later that night she heard a snap in the woods. She leapt to her feet, her spear ready, then proceeded to walk on... *Thump!* She fell to the floor... and Leah was dead! The leader had found her whilst searching for food and now she's dead.

Leah Ounsworth (11)
Cowes Enterprise College, Cowes

Greg

At birth everybody's death date was tattooed on the back of their neck. Mine's dated yesterday! When I reached double digits of age, ten years old. I'm finally allowed to look at my date, I want to see how long I have to enjoy my life. Today is 01/01/1932 - mine's dated yesterday! Oh no...!
This is now Greg's mum writing this story, my poor boy was shot in the foot so he was unable to carry on writing. Six minutes later... "My boy! My boy!" Greg was shot at the hospital with a shotgun! That was the end of Greg.

Harvey J Wheeler (13)
Cowes Enterprise College, Cowes

Away

I stepped into the terminal expecting to see everyone rushing to get their bags, parents hurriedly taking their kids to the toilet though they were already late or that one British businessman wearing a full suit and tie, grumbling about the bags being slow. But, there was no one. No one well, except for a huddle of fifteen-year-olds all looking worried and whispering wildly. I looked behind me and again it looked like all the kids the same age as me were the only people that had got off the plane! Where had everyone gone? Where was my family?

Freddie Newton (12)
Cowes Enterprise College, Cowes

Secrets Of The Basement

There was a noise coming from the basement. I was home alone and my house was not at all safe. I slowly came out of my room. *Bang! Bang! Bang!* The noise startled me and I sprinted back in. My heart was pounding louder and louder. I crept down the stairs, intrigued but terrified. What could the noise be? I finally got down to the basement door and luminous blue light glowed from within. My clammy palm grabbed the ice-cold handle. I prepared myself for whatever could be inside. I pulled down the handle and cautiously opened the door...

Lucy Jane Ashdown (13)
Cowes Enterprise College, Cowes

Blank

The officer lay dead on the floor, a trickle of blood from his skull slowly dripped to the ground. *Drip, drip, drip.* I stepped over his body, prodding him with my foot. He would not wake. Slowly I stumbled out of the terminal, the wind hammering into my face. One child, one girl, only she remains. She must leave. The leaves swirled round me as I tore through the park. Old rubbish littered the ground. I opened my briefcase and threw myself through the window, it clicked shut behind me. I exited, I knew he would not awake ever again...

Jack Jenner (12)
Cowes Enterprise College, Cowes

The Clock Is Ticking

My dark visionaries never left the sturdy metal fence. It hissed and crackled sending small parts of flame onto the dampened grass. I could hear someone whispering my name so softly. It was as if the breeze was the one talking to me. It was very late and I had snuck out wanting to watch and listen to the hypnotic waves it created. However it was cold and my hair had already prickled up. That's when the fence rumbled and toppled over sending sparks onto the rock I sat upon, setting it alight... Standing before me was a horrific nightmare.

Taylor Purrott (13)
Cowes Enterprise College, Cowes

The Hooded Figure

The last thing I remember was kicking and screaming as I was dragged out of my home. Now I am sitting in a facility wondering what is going to happen next. They keep on telling me to forgot my past and live my future. I don't know what that means. I've tried to fight back, but I am slowly forgetting everything I've ever known... Even my parents. "It's time to go," a man said as he strode in. He led me to an abandoned room. A hooded figure stood in front of me. Hands shaking, he slowly lowered his hood...

Macy-Jo Almond (13)
Cowes Enterprise College, Cowes

The Picture

Cleaning your room. What's more boring than cleaning your room? I started cleaning out my cupboard. The majority of stuff was old clothes but then I found the picture. The picture that changed my life. It was just poking out from one of my jacket pockets and was so small it could have possibly just been the label. But this wasn't a label. I could recognise myself in the picture, standing next to two people... A man and a woman. I could only assume them to be my parents, but if they're my parents, who are those people downstairs?

Ryan Simm (13)
Cowes Enterprise College, Cowes

The Basement

There was a noise coming from the basement. What was it? I opened the basement door... *skkrrr*, the door opened. "Hello, anyone down there?" I took a step back. Should I go in? I went in. Slowly I went down the stairs. Quickly turned the light on. There was nothing down in the basement. I slowly walked around the basement. Suddenly I saw a dark shadow. I ran back up the stairs. Yet again the noise was getting louder and louder. The door opened... *boom!* I was very scared. I really hoped it didn't happen again.

Blake Badger (11)
Cowes Enterprise College, Cowes

I Thought I Would Die!

At birth everyone's tattooed with their date of death. Mine's dated yesterday! It was the day before my death not my birthday, my death day. I tried my hardest not to think about tomorrow. I crammed all I could into that day as I knew I wouldn't be around for long... Would I? It was my time to go. My last diary entry, my last hour. I would say wish me luck but I won't be back so goodbye life. I don't understand. I was supposed to die yesterday but I am still here? The injection went wrong! *What's happening?*

Chloe Jessica Harris (12)
Cowes Enterprise College, Cowes

Killer Of The Night

A loud bang echoed through the house... My mum and dad shouted from the bottom of the stairs telling me to stop banging. If I wasn't banging and they weren't then who was it? It hit night and the banging happened again. I knew something was wrong. So I went to check it out. The basement door was open? It's never open... I grabbed a knife and a torch and went down. After taking one step, the banging got louder. I looked round and there was nothing. I was confused about what was going on, until someone grabbed my shoulder...

Reece Pierce (14)
Cowes Enterprise College, Cowes

Untitled

I knew there was something up. Caleb was downstairs. He didn't seem too happy. Ed walked in through the door. Everything was so different. I felt strange knowing I should be dead. They all looked at me, no one took their eyes off me. I looked in the mirror, my skin a pale colour, almost a blue undertone but my body temperature was boiling. Caleb came up to me, holding me tighter than ever. It was as if something had happened. Something bad. I couldn't remember a thing. Turning to Caleb, I saw fear in his eyes. I was terrified.

Abbie Faulkner (13)
Cowes Enterprise College, Cowes

The Day The Baby Cried, I Died

The last thing I remember is the train. It was heading towards me at roughly 160mph. I was sprinting and then I heard the scream... It was the sound of a lady, she was screaming, "My baby!" Behind her I could see a man holding a bundle of white sheets (that were turned red). He also had something in his other hand, I couldn't make it out exactly but I could tell it was some sort of weapon.

"Well it sounds like you had a rather exciting day!" said the angel as my polished coffin was lowered into a grave...

Emma Brown (12)
Cowes Enterprise College, Cowes

Nightmare

For as long as I can remember there has been a monster under my bed. I've always been scared to look but I know he's there. Each night I keep hearing these noises. Every night, they got louder and louder. I'd finally had enough of it. Although I was only eight and petrified, I'd finally picked up the courage and peered under my bed. In horror I shot back up and pulled the covers over my head. Shaking almost to death, these slimy orange, octopus-like tentacles slowly moved over my body. I was sure I was going to die...

Owen Forster (12)
Cowes Enterprise College, Cowes

Nothing

... nothing; nothing at all. The trees around me are dead like my soulless heart. I fear my life. I am lying on my back, weak, barely breathing, staring at the clouds that look motionless too. The vile life form. A shiver goes down my spine, my hair stands on end. The 'thing' approaches me closer and closer. It is extraordinarily slender, sinister too. Its eyes seem to glow red and go through your heart, killing you dead. How am I alive? I am definitely dead. Now I am here, nowhere to be seen, in the unknown. I am nothing.

Rosie Thistlewood (12)
Cowes Enterprise College, Cowes

The Mystery Amulet

At birth everyone's tattooed with their date of death. Mine's dated yesterday... I suppose it's something to do with the earthquake. The last thing I remember is the chicken nuggets falling from the sky and the melted marshmallows flowing like a river. I remember how much I had run through the debris and the rubble. Everything was falling on top of me as I ran. I got to a small pond. It was a light blue crystal colour. Floating on the bottom was a golden amulet. I reached to grab it, snatched it in my hand and I ran...

Izzy Reece (14)
Cowes Enterprise College, Cowes

Birth Tattoos

At birth everyone's tattooed with their date of death. Mine's yesterday. I'll start at the very beginning. It was a blissful, peaceful morning. I was running out the cottage door to catch the school bus. I must have tripped and fallen into the road... I blacked out. All I could hear was the sirens and voices then I woke up. I was absolutely fine. But I had just been run over by the bus. I got up and went to school as normal. On the way home I passed a shop window and the reflection staring back at me wasn't mine.

Kaitlyn McFarlane (12)
Cowes Enterprise College, Cowes

Metaphorical Nightmare

Why does this thing have to happen to me? Only me. This isolation makes the whole atmosphere around me freeze. I feel secluded in my own bubble. Better yet, it's the truth. This entrapment, all these beautiful people, all these bars. How did God come to this? They need to be freed, one way or another. I can't leave. Not now, not ever. When they leave I'll still be here. I'll always be here. Even if science finds a way. Never ever free, how can I? Trapped for life. I pick them and choose them. I am your nightmare.

Tia Kirwin (13)
Cowes Enterprise College, Cowes

The Chosen One

We watched from the space station as the Earth exploded...
A tall man dressed in black held me in chains against a
concrete wall. He repeated the words, "You are the chosen
one," over and over.

As I watched the world shatter all I could think was, *why am
I the chosen one?* I shouted, "Why me?"

Suddenly eleven men in white suits came and told me I was
the child of a hero but also a villain. Today's the day that
they get revenge. Five bullets shot. My body was dead and
yet I was not. Why?

Emily Barrow (13)
Cowes Enterprise College, Cowes

Imposters

They don't look like me. They don't act like me. Who are they? Who am I? My parents are a mystery. They despise me. I want to find out why. I've searched almost every inch of this house for evidence... except here. This had to be it. It seemed suspicious. It was so heavily sealed that even a pocketknife had a hard time tearing open the seal that lined the box. Reaching inside I found a dusty frame wrapped in a stained, white cloth. I unravelled the family portrait; if these are my parents, who's that downstairs?

Nicole Knight (14)
Cowes Enterprise College, Cowes

The Day I Nearly Died

I got off the plane, the terminal was empty. There was nothing to be seen, nothing to be heard but the stench was revolting, inhumane, foul. I felt sick! I wondered into the building, trolleys trashed, suitcases everywhere and nobody, just me and silence. Within a minute of walking in I heard a discomforting shriek, it got louder and louder! Then stopped! I knew I was not alone any more; I could see something, it was a ray, a ray of light getting brighter, too bright to bear. It caressed my skin. Am I in Heaven? Why me? Why me?

Jared Lancaster (14)
Cowes Enterprise College, Cowes

The Infinite Child

One day, I was looking around in my parents' bedroom while they were out and I found a family portrait with me in it and a different set of parents standing next to me. I wanted to see what this was about so I snooped around the attic and found a cloning machine that had my DNA in it. There was a clipboard with prices for occupations: business owners £100, carpenters £250. All clones in cryogenic status. They all looked like me. Hope I'm the original and not a second clone after the other one failed in life.

Samuel Joseph Huckle (13)
Cowes Enterprise College, Cowes

The Unexpected

I began to wonder what could have happened. I had more questions than answers at this point. A bright orange light was flashing faintly at the back. It was at this point I began shivering. I was deaf yet quite confident. Now I carried on making my way towards the exit. The silence made me feel uncomfortable. That's all I ever heard. Deep silence. Suddenly, something gave me a hard blow on the head. I began getting up slowly, and to my surprise, the entrance was blocked off by stones. Was this the end or just the beginning?

Pavel Sorocean (11)
Cowes Enterprise College, Cowes

Untitled

I felt a sudden thud of fear. Questions played on repeat in my mind. What's happened? Why am I alive still? You'd think I'd class myself as lucky, but something's wrong. This is wrong. All my emotions crowded in my chest, making it hard to breathe. I stood up from the chair, I had fallen asleep the previous night, expecting it to be my last. It was a deadly silence. I turned to look at the door. A sense of danger covered me like a coffin. I stood alone in the cold unwelcoming dark. There was a sudden knock...!

Eden Boorman (14)
Cowes Enterprise College, Cowes

The Wrong Family

The question rang in my head. I stole it from their room I don't think they know, not yet. I hear a knock on my bedroom door; I hid the picture behind me.
"Are you okay Honey?" Mum questioned.
Every word disgusted me, now I knew the truth.
"I'm going to bed. I've got a test tomorrow!" She'd gone. I could hear the TV blaring once more. I emptied my school bag and shoved in all I needed. I jumped off the balcony. I was out and all I knew was that I needed to run very far away.

Lili Boon (12)
Cowes Enterprise College, Cowes

The Thing Downstairs

There was a noise coming from the basement. It was two o'clock. I heard a noise, it was a groan. I picked up my Nerf gun and walked downstairs. The door was glowing green so I ran upstairs and hid under my covers.

After a few hours I heard a groan again. So I went into my mum and dad's room and they were gone. I psyched my nerves and went downstairs. I counted to myself, "1, 2, 3." I opened the door and goo splashed on my face...

"April Fool's!"

"Mum and Dad, what...?"

Lewis Giles (13)

Cowes Enterprise College, Cowes

Realising

The floorboards creaked as they unwillingly held my weight upon them. I was expecting it to be quiet but instead I could hear hundreds of different creatures crawling and flying around me. As slowly as possible, I lifted the lid off the chest. *Creak!* I held my breath, hoping that it had not woken my parents, then breathed out; I was safe! I peered into the darkness and there was a picture of me with two adults around me. If these were my real parents then who were those people sleeping downstairs? My heart froze...

Lotti Heathcote (12)
Cowes Enterprise College, Cowes

Killer

I froze. My blood ran cold. I had to get out of here. "Tea's ready!" the untrustworthy voice called up the stairs. I had already packed my bag. Not daring to look back, I jumped. The ground rushed towards me. As soon as I landed. I ran. I didn't know where. I didn't know what I was going to do. I just ran.

"Where are you going?" the chilly voice echoed behind me. I couldn't bear to look back. A cold, firm hand gripped my shoulder and the last cry that could be heard was mine...

Rosie Egerton (11)

Cowes Enterprise College, Cowes

Dragon Vs Water Bottle

There was a noise coming from the basement. It couldn't have been my parents as they were asleep. I went downstairs. I could hear stamping. I opened the door and was freaked out. There was a tiny little dragon. Well it looked like one. The dragon was going crazy. Then a portal appeared. The dragon went through it. I followed. It was not a good place. Fire everywhere! Then I saw a gigantic dragon, it was red. It came straight at me. Then I remembered I had a water bottle. I threw it at the dragon, then got away.

Darcy Philip McBride (12)
Cowes Enterprise College, Cowes

Gone

The airport was packed. Hard to see where you were going. Finally I got on the plane and everything went black. I heard voices but couldn't see the faces. Suddenly my vision came back and no one else was on the plane. I got off and the terminal was empty, deserted like the middle of a desert. There were still noises all around me. It felt like people were touching me, like I was in an upside-down dimension but still on Earth. I turned around and someone was there. It charged for me and slowly ripped my face apart...

Rhys Hall (13)

Cowes Enterprise College, Cowes

Why Am I Alive?

How is this possible? Is the date wrong? Am I destined to live longer or did the cancer that they implanted into my brain at birth not have time to manifest and grow until eventually it burst and I was met with the cold, unforgiving hand of death? Maybe I was like the eternal one. But that was an old wives' tale. Or was it? The eternal one was rumoured to have lived for one hundred thousand years until he was butchered by the government. If that was his fate, what would be mine? Could I be the Earth's saviour?

Samuel Evans-Murray (14)
Cowes Enterprise College, Cowes

His Face...

I got off the plane. The terminal was empty. It was eerily quiet. I slowly walked forward, all of my senses on full alert. Something was wrong, very wrong. My eyes scanned the surroundings and that was when I saw it. One person, right in the middle of the building, just stood there. I quickly walked over to him, something I would soon regret. "Excuse me Sir, but do you know where everyone has gone?" I asked quickly. I was only a few meters away from him. I walked around to see him but then I saw his face...

Ashleigh Jennings (12)
Cowes Enterprise College, Cowes

The One Shot

The last thing I remember is, closing down all the windows and doors and boarding them down. But now my security guard is in the hospital needing surgery. From my office I saw someone across the roof with a sniper, using my mounted telescope, I saw them jolt back. I knew they fired a shot but just in time my security guard jumped in front of me and the bullet hit him... I looked to see if he was okay but he was unconscious so I looked through the telescope. The sniper was gone! Then someone knocked the door loudly...

Dylan James Gould (14)
Cowes Enterprise College, Cowes

Untitled

At birth everyone's tattooed with their date of death. Mine's dated yesterday...
I stared at the ink that stood out on my wrist. The numbers blurred. I had outlived my death date. I was meant to be dead. The world came back into focus as a bullet shrieked past my head. A high-pitched squeal surrounded me. I sank to the floor, clamping my hands over my ears in a struggle to make it stop. I staggered to my feet and ran from them. They were not happy. They were angry, very angry and now I had to survive...

Caitlin Chessell (12)
Cowes Enterprise College, Cowes

Why?

I woke up. It was terrifying. There were at least twenty of us. All lying down in one long row. We were being experimented on. DNA samples being taken from us because we were special. I didn't know that yet. They·made their way down, slowly. I was at the end of the row. But why were we there. It wasn't long before I found out. I was quite surprised. The DNA sample didn't hurt. When they took it I remembered why I was there. Everyone in that room had their death date the day before but had survived. Why?

Bradley Morris (13)
Cowes Enterprise College, Cowes

My Mind?

There was a noise coming from the basement. I felt uneasy. Were my parents home? I lay gazing at the stars on the ceiling that my dad had stuck there years ago. I missed those times terribly! My parents left three nights ago, not uncommon. The noise got louder. Times like this made my mind run wild. I thought about things I didn't want to. I decided to make a brave move and tiptoe across to the bathroom to get a better listen. The light was streaming into my bedroom. I heard the noise again. It was pounding...

Lily Copeland (12)
Cowes Enterprise College, Cowes

Blaze

Drenched in cold sweat. I walked ahead. Every step became harder to handle than the last. My body begged for sleep. My throat for water. This desert seemed to stretch on and on. I needed to follow my compass north. But where was it? I struggled to move my hands up and down my body searching for the one thing that could save my life. It wasn't there. I couldn't go back. No time to search. Every second I wasted was a moment I could die. My only chance was to go forward, guided by quiet sounds of the wind...

Velimira Radoeva Ekova (12)
Cowes Enterprise College, Cowes

Alive And Dead

The last thing I remember was the colour red. It reminded me of pain. Of my arriving death. Yet it also brought warmth. Beginning to relax, I wanted to find a memory of the best time in my life. An image, a name, anything to help me assure myself that my life wasn't wasted. I couldn't find anything. Beads of salty liquid fell from my lashes. A blinding light to carry me onwards filled me with harsh emptiness and despair. My life was over. I felt it. I knew it. But I was awake. I was alive, and dead...

Erin Leah Longford (13)
Cowes Enterprise College, Cowes

The Noise!

There was a noise coming from the basement that sounded like a four-year-old girl crying like she'd dropped her ice cream on a hot summer's day at the beach. When I got closer to the door she said, "Go away!"
I went back upstairs for about ten or twenty minutes watching TV. I heard a door open. Then I went downstairs and saw her close a door while laughing. Then she started crying again. I rang the police. I had no signal. She must have cut the power off. Then I ran out of the house...

Oliver Taylor (14)
Cowes Enterprise College, Cowes

One Night In Nowhere

I get off the plane, the terminal is empty. I turn to see my parents, they're dead. I shuffle forwards like a scared three-year-old girl. A torch blinds me and suddenly there are policemen there. As I pass a haunted zoo I hear a noise. The officers are dead. I run to a creepy house, deathly silence. Suddenly something groans behind me. I turn around. It's going downstairs. I go outside slowly and creep up to the zoo. There is something inside. Then it is gone. But where? Something's behind me...

Josh Fifield (12)
Cowes Enterprise College, Cowes

School Surprise

I discovered this isn't the place that's stated on the map. This place used to be a prison but why, how, who, there must be some mistake. I must investigate. It's a good job I've got a full map of the place. During the day I kept making excuses to leave the classroom. I first started at the bottom of the school, the basement. The door was locked. I picked the lock and barged my way in and went straight to the front of the room. I discovered tubs full of handcuffs. Oh no... what happens next?

Tom Edgecombe (13)
Cowes Enterprise College, Cowes

That's What It Told Me

People look at me like I'm irregular. They stare, point and scowl. They look away and stay back. It wasn't my fault. Why am I alive? I was confused. Why wasn't I dead? I was ready yesterday, it never happened. Now I want to live. No need to live. I have to find out what happened. It was like something was happening and I want know what it was. I don't have to be in the dark anymore. I want to know what is happening on this planet. I live here. I was supposed to die yesterday it told me...

Oliver Thomas Baugh (11)
Cowes Enterprise College, Cowes

My Death Diary...

I need to tell someone the truth, before it's too late. I can't tell. No one can know. I'm not normal and I never will be. All my friends are normal, not me. I don't belong here, I don't exist. My friends are together, I'm alone. My friends shine, I never will. My life is over, my soul lives on. They live on Earth, I live where I want. I don't know if we will ever meet again. It's my fault. I killed myself. I don't exist. I wrote this ten long years ago in my diary...

Cerys Dickinson (13)
Cowes Enterprise College, Cowes

The Creepy Doll, Sitting In The Basement

There was a noise coming from the basement. I was home alone, the only child with no parents to be looked after. I walked down into the basement and saw a creepy doll just sitting there and staring at me. Every direction I walked, the doll's face moved the same way. I was very puzzled and confused. The doll spoke to me and her eyes went ruby red. I ran back up the stairs, opened the door, locked every door. I went to open the kitchen door. The same doll appeared with a knife. I don't know why...

Maddy McPhee (12)
Cowes Enterprise College, Cowes

I Remember!

The last thing I remember, I was in my room and I was seeing black shadows walking through the dark, scary hall with whispering voices as if someone was have a conversation with someone else. I thought I was in a dream thinking that it was not real and that nothing was happening but I was also thinking: *what if it's real? Am I going to die? Is my family safe?* I was so paranoid. My door was wide open so I ran as fast as I could to shut the door. The door creaked and the shadow looked back...

Bethany Marie McPhee (14)
Cowes Enterprise College, Cowes

All Alone

I looked behind me but nobody was there. As I ran back onto the plane, I could hear faint voices. I quickly spun my head around but still, no one was there. Either everyone was hiding from me or I had gone totally insane... What was the point of taking this lousy trip to Orlando if no one was here? I ran around the abandoned airport hoping I could spot someone or something! I dropped my bags and began punching myself. If this was a dream then I could wake up! But no, I had clearly gone totally insane...

Patrick Middle (12)
Cowes Enterprise College, Cowes

Abandoned

I woke not in my normal bed but a strange bed. A hospital bed. How did I get here? Why am I here? I shouted for the nurse. She didn't come. Maybe she didn't hear me. I shouted again. Nothing. So instead of shouting again I stood up, tried to walk, but my legs crumbled. I decided to lean against the wall and find someone but it was empty. I got outside to New York City where once flooded streets were empty. It was just me and the paper boy. I walked around the dystopian city until I saw her...

Jude Van Manton (13)
Cowes Enterprise College, Cowes

The Beast In The Woods

On the 9th November Timothy started sprinting away from his parents into Scratchfield Park. Over night he was showing off to his mates in the pitch-black. He slipped off a rock. He looked above him and saw green, glowing eyes coming from the branch above him. The beast leapt on him and strangled him and put the boy under his arm and ran all the way to his house and put him in bed. His dad saw the crazy animal so Timothy's dad shot the animal. He felt brilliant but the next day he went to prison.

Jack Goring (12)
Cowes Enterprise College, Cowes

Departure

I was coming back from holiday with my son. There were seven other people on the plane. There was a bright light before we landed but no one cared. We landed but no one was at the terminal. Then we noticed the bodies. Then a ragged flight attendant limped out of the shadows screaming. Then behind her was a oozing zombie. I picked up a gun from one of the baddies. The place was nuked and it turned everyone into oozing zombies. My son turned to me with a tear in his eyes. "What happens now?"

Callum Edisbury-Bell (14)
Cowes Enterprise College, Cowes

Test Subject

I sprung up out of my medical bed to wonder how long I'd blacked out? Days? Years? Decades? However long I had been here, I had definitely lost some of my fat, there was a first. I looked down at my hands that were caked in mud and sweat. Why was I here? I looked to the side of me and saw a decaying carcass rotting in the humid heat. Then I saw it, a nuclear power sign. A cracked TV slowly turned on to reveal a man who said, "Congratulations, you have been chosen to be a test subject!"

Toby Ambridge (13)
Cowes Enterprise College, Cowes

Untitled

I panicked, trying to remember who it was downstairs. I walked down praying for my life. I accidentally knocked into my fake mum. She asked, "Why are you in such a rush?"
I replied, "Can I go to the park with my mates?"
"No," my mum snapped.
In my head I was thinking, *I need to get out of here!* That's it, my window. I jumped out my window and rolled away to the neighbour's. I knocked on the door but my fake parents were standing there...

Benjamin Van Der Helstraete (11)
Cowes Enterprise College, Cowes

There Was A Noise Coming From The Basement

I was home alone one night, it was dark outside and a full moon was out. There was no one home and all I was hearing was noises. I kept telling myself that it was nothing. I was wrong, coming from the basement there were things scuffing against the floor and every movement there was a noise. I locked myself into my room and sat in the corner with my head on my knees, waiting for someone to come home. I heard footsteps coming downstairs and barged into my room. I was in danger. I hid under my bed...

Tilly May Butler (13)
Cowes Enterprise College, Cowes

Expiry Date

I have reached my expiry date, like cheese. It has been tattooed on my wrist since birth. We all thought this was our death but in fact it's our ticket to leave this mislead, perfect life. Here they are harvesting us but not like a crop in an open field, we are in a room where you are breathing in everyone else's air. As I look at the people around me I wonder how long they have been here with their wrinkled faces and chapped lips. I know that I can't let anyone else end up like us...

Esme Sheath (13)
Cowes Enterprise College, Cowes

My Basement Of Mannequins

There was a noise coming from the basement so I walked down the stairs and into the basement. The door creaked open and I couldn't see a thing. I flicked the light, *flick!* Nothing. Again, *flick!* Nothing. I got my flashlight and turned it on then right in front of me was a headless mannequin. I moved it out of the way and realised there was a bunch of mannequins around me in a circle. I got freaked out and tried to run out the door but the door was locked. I was trapped!

Freddie Cox (12)
Cowes Enterprise College, Cowes

The Space Station

We watched from the space station as Earth exploded. Imagining the chaos we must have caused made my skin crawl. My eyes darted to my father. There was a glint of evil in his eyes and a smile crept across his scarred face. A shiver shook my spine as I thought of the sick and twisted mind inside my father's head. Am I like him? Will I end up betraying everyone I ever cared about, like he did? All of a sudden all the air was knocked out of me as if my mind was out to brutally kill me...

Anya Wright (13)
Cowes Enterprise College, Cowes

Horrible Halloween

One dark Halloween, John was playing on his Xbox, his mum was out with his little sister. He went downstairs to get something to eat. Then the doorbell rang. He thought it was trick or treaters but there was a letter. John wondered who it could be from? It wasn't a normal letter. I was just a party invitation so he put the date on his calender. He was on his Xbox still. Then he heard a noise in the basement and he was wondering who or what it could be. He found the courage to go...

Kade Woodford (12)
Cowes Enterprise College, Cowes

Terminal Disturbance

I got off the plane, the terminal was empty. I looked back and everybody that had came off the plane was gone. The hairs on my arms started to lift up like a balloon. I saw this figure up in the plane window and I stared and stared. I blinked my eyes for one second and it was gone. I searched for help as I saw it again, it was now running for me. I felt adrenaline. I ran and ran but it caught up to me. It said, "You're dead, you're in Heaven. I will take you to God!"

James Thompson (12)
Cowes Enterprise College, Cowes

The Thing

I need to tell someone the truth before it's too late. I heard the door downstairs open. They were here. I grabbed it and leapt out the window. I climbed onto the roof. The FBI have been after me for hours. I pulled him out of the bag. He was fine. I leapt from house to house, my heart pounding like an African drum. I climbed down the fire escape. I slid into an alley, my skin cold like Lego. I got back on my feet and casually walked out. I exit, a black car pulls up, I get in...

Luke Felstead (14)
Cowes Enterprise College, Cowes

One Shot

The sun is blazing, I take out the map. *I must be close*, I think, staring at the sniper on the back seat. I wonder will I get paid for the contract. It only gave me an hour to kill. I cut the engine as I get close to the house. I can't see any vantage points. I can see twenty-four guards. It needs to be clean. I will only kill them if I have to. After negotiating three guards I have the location of Kim Jong-Un. I approach the bedroom, one shot and he is gone for good...

Liam Parkman (14)
Cowes Enterprise College, Cowes

The Sound Underground

There was a noise from the basement. It sounded like screaming with heavy banging. How could this happen? Nobody was seen going inside for three hours! I tried to be brave, whilst whimpering and shaking. I slowly stepped down the stairs. I dreaded to imagine what could possibly be down there. Should I do this? My head says yes but my heart says no. I reluctantly trust my head and go. But when I get there I am greeted by the most horrific sight I have every seen in my whole life...

James Boxx (12)
Cowes Enterprise College, Cowes

The Narrow Escape!

The last thing I remembered was getting dragged out of my house by my arms and legs. I was kicking and screaming, "Let go of me!" They never did. The next thing I knew my house was up in flames. I shouted, "You saved my life! Thank you!" I gave them a hug. I was wondering where I was going to stay now. I decided to ask them. They said they would help me find a new home to stay while my house was fixed. I was so confused. I don't know how this ever happened!

Lucie Hayden (13)
Cowes Enterprise College, Cowes

The Magical Sun

The sun was blazing. I took out the map, I must be close to the blazing sun that was shining on the silver path. Then I heard a deep voice saying, "Welcome to a magical land. Come and explore Sun Land. What you need to do is stay still and I will make..."
The voice stopped and all went back to normal. I walked to the hotel. When I walked to the hotel the voice came again, so then I knew it wanted to guide me to the hotel and be with me forever. So I was very happy.

Steve Edgcombe (11)
Cowes Enterprise College, Cowes

Strange Noises

There was a noise coming from the basement. Strange creaking noises as if someone was breaking into the basement. I thought it was nothing but then I heard a smash. I stopped what I was doing and went down to the kitchen. I grabbed a sharp knife. The sharpest knife in fact. I carried it down to the basement. Slowly I walked in but it felt like years because I was scared. I reached the basement door and turned the handle. I opened the door and then... That is all I can remember...

Joshua Wilson (12)
Cowes Enterprise College, Cowes

The Noise

I heard a noise coming from the basement. It felt like I had been walking for hours and hours. My hands were ice-cold by the time I got to the door. I opened the old crooked door and walked down the stairs shaking all the way down. I shone my torch and the noise suddenly got much louder. It sounded like a constant banging on the wall and a scratching sound soon after the bang. My mind told me to stop at this point but I had to keep going. As I approached the noise, I froze...

Finn Mahoney (12)
Cowes Enterprise College, Cowes

The Demon Cat

I went to check out the noise. To my surprise there was a kitten with a laundry basket on its head. The little kitty had a pink ribbon and black fluffy fur. But on its head were two little horns. The cat walked up to me. Suddenly, it bolted to the basement door. I chased after it and I found it in the kitchen eating the cake my mum made for her book club. After devouring the cake the little brat came up to me and clawed me on the leg, an odd grin on its face. Then darkness...

Rose Robinson (12)
Cowes Enterprise College, Cowes

Untitled

Why, why was it yesterday? I need to know the truth before it's too late. I have heard of people dying before their day of death but not after. Am I ghost or swapped at birth or what? I'll ask my parents. They told me that I was not swapped at birth and I am definitely still alive, so what? Maybe if I research it I may find the answer. Aaah, no Wi-Fi! *Beep, beep, beep, beep...*
I am so lucky that that was just a dream or I could have been dead already.

Jacob Kennesion (12)
Cowes Enterprise College, Cowes

Am I Dead Or Alive?

I am lying on the floor with a broken spine, blurry eyes and a fractured skull. My ears are full of blood and gravel. I try to stand up. I fall to my knees. Lying around me, not just dead bodies but massive destruction. The memories start coming back to me. I was walking out a shop then this weird man blew up and that was all I remember, but where are my mum and my dad and my family? Am I dead or alive? My eyes shut, I stop breathing. I gasp for air. Where am I now? Dead...

Isobel Irene Cole (13)
Cowes Enterprise College, Cowes

Remember

The last thing I remember is walking down the street and everything else was blacked out from history. I was lying in a room, a dark room. I slowly walked towards the door in the corner. I got to the door. I opened the door. I looked out, no one was there. I was alone. I started walking to the hall. I was panicking then I found a lonely-looking boy. I walked down the hall and there were all the townsfolk hiding. There was a war going on. I got hit so went far away to live.

Molly Carter (13)
Cowes Enterprise College, Cowes

Dream

I walk out of my bedroom into the kitchen to get some ice cream. I can see red stuff coming out of the cupboard so I open the cupboard door and I scream. There is a hand in there. I run to find someone but I can't find anyone. I go into my sister's bedroom. She is not in there. I open her cupboard because there is red stuff coming out of there. Her body is just lying there. Then I hear a massive bang. I go downstairs and I see Mum. She has a gun... *Bang!*

Nakita Eleanor Munn (13)
Cowes Enterprise College, Cowes

Robot Takeover!

I woke up with dirt and rubble all over me. The building I was next to, now only had three walls left. The air was dusty and I couldn't see more than fifty metres. My clothes had no colour as they were faded with dust and also ripped. What was before a luxurious American city, is now nothing more than a wasteland with piles of rubble on every corner. The army was getting weaker every day. The robots were winning. The Earth is now an intergalactic no-man's-land.

Rylan Agius Schembri (13)
Cowes Enterprise College, Cowes

The Dead Man

The sun was blazing. I must be close. I was exhausted. I took one step in the hot sand as I walked along the Sahara Desert. Suddenly a bony hand grabbed my ankle. My life flashed before my eyes. I started to sink. I moved my other foot and another hand snatched it. I gasped as I felt the sun getting hotter. I thought I was going to die but then, there he was in the distance. I heard a voice. "Go! Go!" it said. It was only then I realised that he was dead...

Mia Topping (12)
Cowes Enterprise College, Cowes

The Scary Terminal

I got off the plane, the terminal was empty. I thought it was strange that no one was there. I had to wait for the next plane so I just sat in the café with no workers in sight. I was sitting down and on my phone, then all the lights started to flicker and there were strange shadows. Then I noticed all these dead people on the floor all around me. Then there were gunshots. I panicked and ran as fast as I could to a random plane and got on it...

Megon Blow (12)
Cowes Enterprise College, Cowes

There Was A Noise Coming From The Basement

I crept down the stairs and right in front of me there was a shadow of a grown man. He had something in his hand. All of a sudden it had gone and I heard my little brother scream and I ran up the stairs and saw blood on his bed. I fell to the floor and passed out. Then all I remember is waking up in the hospital. I looked at my hand and it was gone. I heard the doctors saying, "We will have to amputate the arm..."

Kira Plant (13)

Cowes Enterprise College, Cowes

The Couple Downstairs

While searching through the attic, I find some old photos and my birth certificate. I look at the certificate puzzled. I'm the daughter of a famous archaeologist! The first photo I pull out is of my parents getting married, me in their arms. In the second photo, I'm probably three and in a machine. In the corner, my parents lie dead on the floor. Wait... the woman downstairs is the same one operating the machine in the photo. The couple downstairs... if they aren't my parents, who are they?

Bea Jane (12)
King Edward VI Community College, Totnes

Fright Night

My shocking surprise happened on 13th October. I was walking and saw a sign so I wondered if it could be a shortcut home. The trees got taller and thicker, the branches were reaching out. I was lost! Looming ahead was a house with sharp broken windows. The first room. I saw a photo on the mantelpiece of an old Tudor hag with sparse straw hair and coal-black eyes. Feeling eerily alone, I took a step back and the woman slowly got closer. I tried to run but she grabbed me. Everything went black...

Freya Kissane Dilloway Cashman (12)
King Edward VI Community College, Totnes

The Book Of Fears

It was truly a nightmare. Clouds and storms were ganging up on us. Lightning slapped the rain while the trees tripped over with a colossal thud! The shore broke as the salty air filled our nostrils. The tornadoes marched down throughout the city. Monsters of your worst nightmares invaded the land. They warned me not to unlock it. And this was all my fault. Why did I open the tomb? Why?

Emma Tibbetts (12)
King Edward VI Community College, Totnes

Darkness

I thrash about under the bedclothes. All I see is darkness, all I taste is fear, all I hear is the deep, dark beyond. I stumble around, searching for the light switch I know is there, somewhere. My hand brushes the cold plastic and my heart leaps. I go to switch it on, but a hand is already there...

Ella Wyett (13)
King Edward VI Community College, Totnes

To Anyone Who Finds This

Anyone who is reading this I have something to say... I'm Alden Tabor one of the twelve protectors of the universe. I'm also the greatest scientist of this time. I was testing a wardrobe-like dimensional transporter so I could finally prove the existence of infinite universes, infinite choices of what you could do. Some are so opposite that you don't see any difference in theirs and your own. Anyway, I activated it and suddenly out came 200 galaxies worth of armies, all squid humanoids. Now they are after us, then they'll be after our own universe and then get others.

Alden Landis Tabor (11)
St Wilfrid's School, Exeter

The Delirious World

A hundred words to tell you my story. The Earth will explode in six months. The government's solution, leave the 50% less intelligent population on Earth. I'm in the 50% intelligent population, but I don't believe it. I don't want to. All the countries the government loathes are staying behind. I am the president's son, but my mum is staying behind. I'm sorry Mum.

Six months later. Five, four, three, two, one... and that is it. We watched the Earth explode from the space station. I will never have faith in humanity again. But I will avenge. I will.

David Antwi (12)
St Wilfrid's School, Exeter

My Wonderful Journey

I looked around me left and right. Suddenly, I heard a weird growling noise, I didn't know what it was. I ran. It was getting dark and I still hadn't found the gold. "It's weird," I said. I have come across some nice creatures on the way, bears, lions, snakes and wild birds. I was scared because it was so dark. I saw an elephant, he saw me. He started to run at me. I was horrified. I started to hide. Luckily he didn't see me but I was still on my journey to find the gold. Until next time...

George Nicholas Sparey (12)

St Wilfrid's School, Exeter

The Creature At The Airport

We got off the plane. The terminal was deserted. As I looked behind me, no one was there. Walking past the empty passport control made me shiver but footsteps could be heard. A monster was slithering near me. It came to me and tried suffocating me. I escaped and ran like a cheetah. An eerie scream from the creature made me run faster. I reached the airport doors and charged through them like a rhino. I ran to the nearest taxi. I was safe but the door locked on me as I realised who was driving. It was the monster...

Tim Allison (14)
St Wilfrid's School, Exeter

She Murdered Herself

I came back from work, I went in the kitchen and found my wife lying down on the floor playing with the puppy. I didn't speak to her, I just walked out of the kitchen and I went to the television. I was hungry so I went in the kitchen and late at night I found my wife weeping at the kitchen table. I asked why she was crying. She showed me the bloody knife in her hand. "No matter what I do, you won't stay dead." The next day I woke up, my wife was dead...

Olivia Richardson (11)
St Wilfrid's School, Exeter

Weird Things

I walked in a direction but I went the wrong way, so I went the right way. It was so hot as if I was in a desert. I had no water after I drank the last bit about five minutes ago. I was finally there. All of a sudden I got teleported to a place with no one there. I screamed for help but there was no reply. I saw a black teleporter over the hills and I walked to it and I went in the black teleporter. I was at the place I wanted to be.

Christian Tigwell (12)
St Wilfrid's School, Exeter

Viewpoint

There was a noise coming from the basement. Just yesterday our fingers brushed the Ouija board keeping the gathering from turning lifeless: today, the noises started. The enchanting blood spilt yesterday appeared immortal, bonding five friends for the rest of eternity - but how far could the magic of immortality stretch? The floorboards breathed as the dull thudding stretched the house and I cautiously crept to the crevices of the cellar. My sadistic grin spread across my face with anticipation as my hand caressed the doorknob before catching it in my clutches. The door creaked open; suddenly I could see...

Annie West (16)
The John Of Gaunt School, Trowbridge

Time Is Money

At birth everyone's tattooed with their date of death. Mine's dated yesterday. I'm supposed to be dead but I'm not. You see I've lived for so long that they have actually changed the system now. You work for time and you pay with time. So my tattoo is probably worthless. I have three days to live but I don't want to get another loan for another ten years because I'll only have to pay it back again. I remember I am already in debt. *Wham!* the door went. It was the cops! Before I knew it my life was drained...

Ryan Bedford (13)
The John Of Gaunt School, Trowbridge

The Isolated Airport

I got off the plane, the terminal was empty. My footsteps echoed through the isolated building. Where was everyone? Dead? No. Surely not. Looking around I saw the shops, not even closed, but left in a hurry. It seems to be evacuated. Just then I realised that everyone I was on the plane with had gone too. Oh God. I was so scared. What on Earth was happening? I could hear loud noises, drowning the sound of footsteps. I covered my ears with my hands. The wall I was facing exploded before my eyes. A huge plane charged towards me...

Ethan Clark (12)
The John Of Gaunt School, Trowbridge

A Dream Or Reality?

The last thing I remember is a party full of happiness and joy. I'm with my family having fun. Then all of a sudden a cold, high-pitched maniacal laugh is heard. Next, I'm on the floor, pain in my arm. All hope is lost till a blazing light is seen in the sky. A warm sweet light and the aroma of roses fills the air. I wake in the orphanage sweating. I still hear the maniacal laugh ringing in my ears. I think and wonder in my head over and over again, *was that a dream, memory, premonition or destiny?*

Amera Mohamed (12)
The John Of Gaunt School, Trowbridge

The Death Tattoo

At birth, everyone's tattooed with their date of death. Mine's dated yesterday... I stare at the window. All I can hear is the clock ticking. It seems easy. Too easy. I stare at my arm. It says the same as it always has. 09/11/17. Today is the tenth... This feels uncomfortable. All I know is that I have to get out of here. I silently get off my chair and leave. I can hear my heart beating in my head, as if I should turn back. I tell myself, no. What should I do? Time is running out!

Sophie Smith (11)
The John Of Gaunt School, Trowbridge

Est.1991

YOUNG WRITERS INFORMATION

We hope you have enjoyed reading this book – and that you will continue to in the coming years.

If you're a young writer who enjoys reading and creative writing, or the parent of an enthusiastic poet or story writer, do visit our website **www.youngwriters.co.uk**. Here you will find free competitions, workshops and games, as well as recommended reads, a poetry glossary and our blog.

If you would like to order further copies of this book, or any of our other titles, then please give us a call or visit **www.youngwriters.co.uk**.

Young Writers
Remus House
Coltsfoot Drive
Peterborough
PE2 9BF
(01733) 890066
info@youngwriters.co.uk